D1172218

What They Said about *A Boys First Diary*

A Boy's First Diary is Glenn Currie's third and strongly
recommended book . . . A unique lyrical voice.
The Midwest Book Review

Currie is blessed with amazing recall. With seeming
ease, he summons up his life as a ten year old
. . . In this book, he outdoes himself.
New Hampshire Magazine

I finished (*A Boy's First Diary*) this afternoon and I am
still laughing. It would make a great weekly sitcom.
Anita Hickey, Book Swap Café

I absolutely loved it . . . Glenn K. Currie has captured the ten-year-
old soul in all of us in his collection . . . titled *A Boy's First Diary*.
Regina Nervo, fifth grade teacher, Long Beach, CA

Dear Mr. Currie: You are the greatest writer in the world.
Jeffrey, Age 10

Dear Mr. Currie: I LOVE YOUR BOOK SO MUCH!
Your #1 fan, Bizzy, Age 10

Surviving Seventh Grade

A sequel to *A Boy's First Diary*

**Glenn K.
Currie**

To Laura and Jack
I hope you have tons fun with
these little stories,

With best wishes,
Glenn K. Currie

Snap Screen Press
CONCORD, NEW HAMPSHIRE

ISBN 978-0-9779675-7-5
Library of Congress Control Number: 2012918850

Designed and composed in ITC Goudy Sans at Hobblebush Books, Brookline, New Hampshire
www.hobblebush.com

Printed in the United States of America

Published by:
Snap Screen Press
6 Dwinell Drive
Concord, NH 03301

For more information, visit the website at:
www.snapscreenpress.com
or e-mail: glenn.snapscreen@gmail.com

*This book is dedicated to America's teachers.
The people who spend their lives helping prepare
us to live in a rapidly changing world.
We may not fully appreciate the influence they
have on our lives when we are thirteen, but
what we learn from them will help determine,
in many ways, the path of our adult lives.
Most of us remember the names of the really
good ones, long after other memories have faded
away. A personal thank you to all the teachers
who put up with me in my teenage years, and
a thank you to teachers everywhere for their
patience, understanding and dedication.*

Contents

Introduction   ix

First Day of School   1

Miss Buxby   2

Class Assignments   3

Woodenhead   4

The Cafeteria   5

The Cafeteria Tables   6

Denard   7

Puppy Love   8

Gym Class   9

Turning Thirteen   10

Lead Belly   11

Lead Belly's Revenge   12

The Hall Monitor   13

The Chipmunk   14

Government Work   15

Girls' Gym   16

Sculls Forever   17

Leeches   18

Pimples   19

Nuclear Attack   20

Locker Room Revenge   21

Brylcreem   22

Yogurt   23

Cockroaches   24

Talking to Girls   25

Football   26

Boxing Starts   27

Thursday   28

Talking About Girls   29

The Talk   30

Parents   31

French Class   32

Asking Becky to the Sock Hop   33

Civics Class   34

American Bandstand   35

Current Events   36

The Dance   37

Basketball   38

After Basketball   39

The Dairy Queen   40

Dress Codes   41

Band Uniforms   42

The Constitution   43

Braindead Baxter   44

Singing at Assembly   45

Relationships   46

Kleenex and Potatoes   47

Bananas   48

Big Molly's Revenge   49

High School Football   50

Awards   51

The Kissing Fight   52

Butchy Talks with Arnold   53

The Becky Fight   54

Report Cards   55

Making up with Becky   56

The Debate   57

The Rope Climb   58

Rope Climb-the Day After   59

What Girls Want   60

Second Base   61

Bras   62

Other Thoughts on Girl Stuff   63

The Sex Lecture   64

French Kissing   65

The Real Sex Lecture   66

Dunking Mr. Foster   67

Charles Atlas   68

The Halloween Dance   69

Locker Inspection   70

B Flat   71

Washed Up   72

Bad Breath   73

The Orchestra   74

Puppies and People   75

The Old Guy   76

Batman vs Superman   77

Where the Girls Are   78

The Snowball Fight   79

Arnold   80

Braces   81

Billy's Accident   82

Drugs   83

Saved by the Paper   84

The Truce   85

The Project   86

Meeting at My House   87

We Discuss Snobby Donna   88

Menstruation   89

The Project Grade   90

Donna's Recital   91

Conclusion   92

Introduction

This book is a work of fiction.
Some of these incidents happened to me,
Some have been described to me by others.
None of the characters, except me, are real.

If your name happens to be
Snobby Donna or Lead Belly or Woodenhead,
It is just a coincidence.
It's not about you.

Many of the characters are the same
As those in *A Boy's First Diary*,
Which is about life
In the fourth grade.

There are hardly any pictures in this book.
If you need illustrations
To get you to open a book,
You are too young to read this.

This book is only for bigger kids
Who understand stuff about girls,
And other things you learn
When you get older.

There are stories in here
About leeches and chipmunks,
And bras and bananas.
It is seventh grade stuff.

The photos above represent characters in this book. Many of you know some kids in your school who look sort of like these pictures. One of the pictures is actually of me. You probably won't be able to guess which one right away.

First Day of School

I'm not sure I like 7th grade.
A whole group of new kids
Are in classes with us.
Some of them are pretty scary.

Three boys in my homeroom shave already.
And they smoke out back sometimes.
One of them, Arnold, called me over before school.
He gave me a really hard noogie on the arm.

He said from now on, when I see him,
I should come over and say hello.
I should also give him something
From my lunch bag each morning.

Then he gave me another hard noogie.
I can hardly move my right arm.
He did the same thing to Marvin
And a couple of the other kids.

I wish Butchy was still in my class.
He started shaving in the 4th grade.
I told Mom to pack extra fruit in my lunch.
She thinks I really like fruit.

Miss Buxby

Arnold came in late to homeroom today,
And started mouthing off to Miss Buxby.
Miss Buxby is old, and she's big and mean.
She grabbed Arnold by the ear.

They went out in the hall
And slammed a bunch of lockers.
When they came back, Arnold was quiet.
Miss Buxby said they were inspecting lockers.

Since she was old, I asked Mom
If she remembered Miss Buxby from school.
Mom gave me "the look" but said everybody does.
She once shut a kid in a locker for four hours.

Mom said they don't do that stuff anymore.
The school has new rules.
I wish they had the old rules for Arnold.
I'm starting to like Miss Buxby.

Class Assignments

At home room on our first day
They assigned us to division levels.
Billy was put in the business section.
I got assigned to the college group.

It is the class from hell.
The only one I know is Snobby Donna.
The kids are really smart and we get lots of homework.
I got assigned the Snob as my lab partner.

Snobby Donna has been my archenemy since 4th grade.
She is "Miss Perfect" and all the teachers love her.
Her parents are really rich
And she looks like a Hollywood model.

She drives me crazy.
Even in science lab she ignores me,
And does the projects the way she wants.
And it's always right.

Woodenhead

Our principal's name is "Woodenhead" Wilson.
Nobody seems to know how he got the nickname.
But he's been there about a hundred years,
So I asked Mom.

She said the spelling got changed.
He always said stuff like
"I wouldn't do that if I were you," or
"Wouldn't it be nice if...."

He used "wouldn't" so much
That the kids started calling him "Wouldn't head."
And pretty soon it became "Woodenhead."
I don't think he likes the nickname.

The Cafeteria

I'm glad I bring my lunch.
When we go to the cafeteria,
All the cool kids
Carry their trays with one hand.

A metal tray with plates and a drink
Is not that easy to carry
With just one hand.
Only girls and nerds use two hands.

We decided we didn't like
The food they serve, anyway.
Who wants fish sticks,
Squash and peach cobbler?

Sometimes they also serve stuff like
Mystery meat and tapioca pudding.
The only thing Billy and I get is milk.
We can carry that with one hand.

The Cafeteria Tables

Billy and I were sitting at lunch yesterday
When this huge shadow
Blocked out the light.
It was an angry shadow.

Denard is a ninth grader.
He plays guard on the school football team.
He said we were sitting
At his table.

It's not good for nerds
To sit at Denard's table.
It's even worse for seventh grade nerds.
He said he wouldn't kill us this time.

Only Denard's friends
Sit at his table.
He said that we
Were definitely not his friends.

We found out that seventh graders
Are only supposed to sit
At the tables farthest from the food line
And closest to the bathrooms.

This is because the bathroom smells
Are worse than the food smells,
Although it's a toss-up
When they serve "excrement on a shingle."

Denard

On the way home from school,
We were still talking about Denard.
Ninth graders aren't supposed
To be that big.

Billy said we should call him "Bluto."
Popeye would need to eat
A lot of spinach
To handle that guy.

I said I heard a rumor
That last year he made
Two seventh graders disappear,
Because they were blocking his locker.

The janitor found them
In two gym lockers
A couple of hours after school.
They were only wearing underpants.

We decided to call him Denard,
And stay out of his way.
If you got shut up in the wrong gym locker,
The fumes might kill you.

Puppy Love

I saw Mary Jane today.
She broke my heart in fourth grade.
She's still pretty tall
And I'm still not so tall.

But I think I'm growing on her.
Before, she thought I was too short.
But when I said "hi" today,
She smiled and waved.

Dad said, when she first broke my heart,
That it was just puppy love.
It was a stage everyone goes through
When they're growing up.

I still don't understand
Why they call it puppy love.
People usually love puppies,
Especially when they're small.

Gym Class

We have gym classes twice a week.
We're all mixed back together for gym.
Arnold and his friends are in my class.
I'm one of the smallest kids.

We had the rope climb today.
You get on a big knot at the bottom of the rope,
And then you're supposed to climb to the ceiling.
I never really got off the knot.

If we didn't climb to the ceiling
We had to do extra push-ups
And run five laps around the gym.
Arnold climbed to the ceiling.

Mr. Foster said that next month
We are going to have boxing classes.
Arnold smiled at me.
I think Mr. Foster hates me.

Turning Thirteen

I turned thirteen today.
I'm officially a teenager.
I told Mom and Dad
That now, I'm practically an adult.

Mom said we were all in trouble,
And hopes she survives.
Dad said thirteen is an unlucky number,
And so are fourteen through nineteen.

I'm not sure what they meant,
But I don't think
They're as excited as I am
About my new status.

My sister, Roxana, is ten.
She said she couldn't wait
To be a teenager, too.
My folks didn't seem excited about that, either.

Lead Belly

Mr. Ledbesson is a math teacher.
We call him "Lead Belly"
Because his stomach hangs out
Way over his belt.

Yesterday he walked into class
With about eight sheets of toilet paper
Hanging out behind him.
Nobody told him.

He always does his classes standing up.
So he didn't find out until third period.
Today Billy snuck in early
And put a roll of toilet paper on his desk.

Lead Belly's Revenge

Lead Belly was in a really bad mood
After the toilet paper thing.
He wanted to know
Who left the roll of TP on his desk.

He said everyone would get detention
If they didn't tell him who did it.
Then he handed out sheets of paper
For everyone to answer secretly.

Billy said he wrote "the Toilet Paper Fairy" on his.
But four kids ratted Billy out.
Billy is in big trouble.
Lead Belly doesn't seem to have a sense of humor.

Billy got detention for a week,
And has to spend the time
Cleaning out the boys' bathrooms.
Some of those toilets are pretty gross.

The Hall Monitor

Snobby Donna is a hall monitor.
When we go to different classes
We're supposed to stay to the right,
Stay in line and move along quickly.

We're not supposed to switch lanes
Except when we get to our class.
I saw Billy in the other lane,
And switched to talk to him.

The Snob started yelling to stay in line.
So Billy and I started switching
Every time we went by her.
Pretty soon lots of kids were doing it.

She was having a super snit.
Then Lead Belly saw us.
We got sent down to Woodenhead.
Arnold snarled at us in detention.

The Chipmunk

Billy and I decided to get even
With Snobby Donna for detention.
We always hear her practicing piano
When we go by her house.

Billy had captured a chipmunk
That was living under his steps,
So we waited until she was practicing
And snuck up to an open window.

We let the chipmunk out of the box
And then hid in the bushes.
There was a lot of screaming
And no more practicing.

Today we put a picture of a chipmunk
In her desk before school.
She turned right around and looked at me.
I just smiled and waved.

Government Work

Mrs. McGann is our Civics teacher.
She has been teaching us how government works.
We've been learning about checks and balances
And the three parts of government.

She says this keeps government
From acting too hastily,
And makes the politicians
Think harder about the laws they pass.

I asked Dad what he thought
About checks and balances.
He said he and Mom
Talk about that all the time.

He said most politicians don't think
And neither do the voters.
People go to Washington
When they can't get a real job.

Mrs. McGann says my Dad was just joking.
They are in charge of writing the country's checks,
And making the laws we live by.
I still don't understand who makes it all balance.

Girls' Gym

There was a big problem at school yesterday.
Miss Buxby caught Arnold and his friends
Hanging out under the stairs
At the end of the building.

They had "found" a hole in the frosted glass
That overlooks the girls' locker room.
She called Woodenhead down,
And he got really upset.

There is a lot of detention in Arnold's future.
The word got around fast
About which girls looked really good.
Today the hole was all boarded up.

Sculls Forever

There's a scary gang of ninth graders.
They call themselves the "sculls."
They all have leather jackets
With the club name on the back.

They also wear thick leather garrison belts.
They sharpen the belt buckles
So that in fights, they can take them off,
And use them as weapons.

The total IQ of the six of them is about 45.
They also have tattoos on their right arms
That say "sculls forever,"
With a skull under it.

Everyone's afraid to mention
That they spelled skull wrong.
Billy dared me to tell them
What a good-looking "crew" they are.

For once in my life,
I decided to keep my mouth shut.
I have enough problems
With seventh graders.

Leeches

Billy and I went swimming today
Up at Dike's Pond.
The water is pretty dirty
And we came out with leeches on us.

We picked the leeches off each other.
Billy even had one on his butt.
He had to pick that one off himself.
We had eight of them.

I had a Junior Mint box
In my backpack.
We ate the candy.
And put the leeches in the box.

I took the box home
And put it in my freezer,
In the back where Mom wouldn't see it.
We're saving it for a special occasion.

Pimples

I had a big pimple on my nose
When I woke up today.
Girls can cover them up a little,
But there's not much boys can do.

Mom still made me go to school,
Even though I looked like Godzilla.
Billy said, if it gets any bigger,
It could explode and kill people.

I didn't want Snobby Donna to see me.
Pimples are afraid to get on her face.
She's always perfect.
Maybe I could explode on her.

I felt a little better
When I saw Becky.
She had a bunch of pimples,
Even though they were covered up a little.

Everything is harder in seventh grade.
You get too many teachers,
A lot of mean kids and too much homework.
And then you get pimples.

Nuclear Attack

We had an atom bomb drill today.
When the bell went off
We all had to get under our desks.
I wonder who thought that up.

I don't like to think about nuclear attacks.
We don't seem to be well-prepared.
If my desk is the best protection we have,
We're in a lot of trouble.

Marvin's dad built a bomb shelter.
Dad says we'll just go there.
I think most of the town
Plans to do that.

I told Marvin to make sure
They have a TV for us to watch,
And they don't serve beans
To such a big crowd.

We don't want to survive
An atom bomb attack
And die from a massive dose
Of poison gas.

Locker Room Revenge

The girls got their revenge last week.
A bunch of us were in the locker room.
Mr. Foster always makes us take a cold shower
When we have finished workouts.

Big Molly threw open the door
And took a picture with her flash camera.
I was lucky, I was down the other end,
She only got part of my butt.

But Arnold was right by the door,
And turned around when the door opened.
The picture was all over school today,
And the girls keep calling Arnold "Wee Willie."

Big Molly didn't even get in trouble.
Mr. Foster was in his office at the time,
And none of the boys wanted to admit
Who got them.

Brylcreem

All the cool kids put Brylcreem in their hair
It's supposed to make them look "debonair,"
But they leave a trail of grease
Everywhere they go.

They're always running combs
And their hands through their hair,
Then stuff gets all over
Doorknobs, desks, and lockers.

In the ads, they show a beautiful girl
Running her hands
Through the hair of some guy
Who looks like he just survived an oil spill.

I always wonder where she puts her hands
After she rubs his head.
I guess it doesn't make any difference
If she's cute enough.

I tried it once but no one rubbed my head.
I didn't know what to do with my greasy comb.
I finally rubbed it off on Snobby Donna's back,
When we were in a crowd.

Yogurt

Big Molly and Belinda
Were eating yogurt at lunch.
This is a perfect example
Of why girls are weird.

When I got home I asked Mom
What is yogurt?
She said it's made from fermented milk,
And then they add bugs to it.

Apparently the bugs are still alive
When they eat the stuff.
The girls said they lose weight eating it.
I can believe that part.

Billy and I were thinking that we should go
To Drooley's and catch some cockroaches.
His apartment has lots of them. We could
Catch some and put them in a bottle of milk.

Then we could bring it to school
And give it to the girls.
I bet that would help them lose
Even more weight.

Cockroaches

Mom wouldn't give us any milk
To put cockroaches in,
So we came up
With a new plan.

Billy has a friend in shop, Moe,
Who actually sometimes eats cockroaches.
We figured this was a valuable skill
That we should make use of.

I paid Moe a quarter
To come with us to lunch today
And sit with big Molly and Belinda.
We brought live cockroaches in a match box.

Moe took one out and started eating it.
The back half of it was still squirming.
The girls were so upset
They tipped over the table.

Unfortunately, the other cockroaches
Got away when the table tipped.
We squished a couple
But they were pretty fast.

Miss Johnson, who runs the cafeteria,
And Woodenhead were both pretty upset.
Moe, Billy and I are getting detention.
Moe says I owe him another quarter.

Talking to Girls

I never know what to say to girls.
Most of them are idiots
When it comes to sports,
And don't know much about super heroes.

They always want to talk about
Clothes, movies stars
And romantic stuff
That makes me want to throw up.

Mom says girls are more sensitive,
but so far two of them
Have punched me in the stomach,
And one said I was too short.

If they weren't cute,
They'd have nothing going for them.
Dad says girls are like new shoes,
They look good but give you blisters.

Football

Billy and I played football after school today.
A bunch of us met at a vacant lot
Near where Sonny lives.
Some of the kids had helmets.

I thought it was touch football.
But it was tackle.
Sonny said not to worry,
It was a friendly game.

I was playing defense
When Thumper Savage ran with the ball.
He came around my side
And I tried to tackle him.

I never knew about straight arms.
He punched me in the face
And ran for a touchdown.
I got a bloody nose and a headache.

Billy said we needed to get helmets like Thumper.
Then we would do better.
I told him my football career was over
Unless I got a lot bigger.

Boxing Starts

Well, the dreaded days have arrived.
A boxing ring was set up in the middle of the gym.
On Tuesday Mr. Foster showed us
How to feint and jab and dance around.

Today he started putting people in the ring.
Everyone has to box a 3-minute round.
Arnold and Wendell did it today.
Wendell got a bloody nose.

Henry's nickname is the "Mad Farter"
Cause he eats beans for breakfast.
Nobody calls him that to his face.
He doesn't like it and he's pretty big.

I am scheduled to box Henry next Thursday.
Arnold told him I used his nickname, and
Henry gave me the "you are dead meat" look.
I plan to be sick next Thursday.

Thursday

Mom wouldn't let me be sick today.
I told her I would definitely be sick tomorrow.
Billy said I was quicker than Henry,
So just dance around and stay away.

Billy made me feel a little better,
But then he asked
If he could have my Boy Scout knife,
If I didn't make it.

Mr. Foster gave me gloves as big as my head,
And a helmet that kept falling over my eyes.
The ring looked pretty small.
Not a lot of running room.

Three minutes is a long time in a boxing ring.
I mostly put the gloves in front of my face.
I tried to run away but got cornered,
And managed to hit Henry in the groin.

That caused a huge fart and everyone laughed.
Henry was really mad after he recovered.
The last minute took about an hour.
I got a fat lip and my ears are ringing.

I hate gym.

Talking about Girls

Billy and I talk about girls more lately.
Some of them are pretty cute.
We might even try to get dates to the school dance,
Although neither of us knows how to fast dance.

They call it a sock hop,
Because everyone takes their shoes off
So you don't ruin the gym floor.
I told Billy he would need to wear clean socks.

His sneakers always smell like wet dog,
And the socks in his locker give off yellow fumes.
Billy said he had a clean pair at home
That he was saving for a special occasion.

He's got a thing for Irma Lawson.
She's the only girl in school who elected to take
Shop instead of home economics,
And she made him a wooden box for his baseball cards.

The Talk

Dad tried to talk to me today about girls.
He said to stay away from them
Until I was twenty-one.
That was pretty much the whole conversation.

I said I already knew a lot of stuff
From listening to the big kids
When we used to play ball
Down behind Emerson School.

I said the only thing I was really unclear about
Was something called "mens truation."
I asked him what it was
And what did it have to do with men.

Dad suddenly remembered some work he had to do.
He said we would talk later.
I think he was going to ask Mom.
I don't think he knows either.

Parents

My parents are too old
To remember much about seventh grade.
Mom remembers some of the teachers,
But she thinks seventh grade was fun.

She must have been one of the cool kids.
They're the only ones who have fun.
I'm sure Dad was a nerd,
He knows even less about girls than I do.

I think when parents get over 30,
They start to forget stuff.
Once you get old like that,
You go downhill pretty fast.

French Class

I hate French class.
I never know what they're saying.
So I just say "Oui" when they ask a question.
Yesterday, that didn't work so well.

I think Miss Dupuis was wise to me.
She asked if my head was made of cheese.
And I said "Oui."
Now all the kids call me "cheese head."

The only good part about that class
Is I sit one row back and one seat over
From Snobby Donna.
I find lots of ways to annoy her.

Yesterday I got her in trouble.
I hit her with a spitball
And she turned around.
The teacher told her to pay attention.

I also like it
When she wears a sleeveless blouse.
Even though I really hate her
She's pretty cute.

Asking Becky to the Sock Hop

I finally worked up the courage
To ask Becky to the dance.
She said yes!
My Dad is going to drive us.

Becky is really nice to me.
She's pretty cute but shy, like me.
She's on the Pep Squad
And plays field hockey.

I don't know why she said yes,
I'm basically a nerd.
I've been rehearsing things to talk about,
But whenever I see her, I say stupid stuff.

I took some dance lessons a while ago,
But everyone dances fast at sock hops.
They don't do cha-chas and fox trots.
Billy says just move my butt and nod my head.

I tried that in front of the mirror,
But I looked like a broken bobblehead.
I don't know why I take advice from Billy,
He doesn't know how to dance either.

Civics Class

We studied integration in civics class today.
Brown v. the Board of Education.
We read stories about a bunch of southern Democrats
Standing at the schoolhouse doors.

They had guns and clubs
And scared the little kids.
The colored students finally got into school
But no one looked happy.

Dad says the whole thing goes back to the Civil War.
They still have a bunch of hooded guys down there,
Called the Ku Klux Klan.
They hate Negroes, Jews, Catholics and Republicans.

They make the Negroes
Use separate bathrooms and water fountains,
Try to keep them from voting,
And make them ride in the back of buses.

Suddenly I didn't feel so bad
Having to deal with Arnold.
At least I know who the bad guys are,
And I can use the regular bathrooms.

American Bandstand

Everybody watches American bandstand
To learn the new dances,
But they keep changing them.
I can never remember the differences.

It's like learning a sport
Where they change the rules
In the middle of the game,
And they never write them down.

They have slops, bops, hully-gullies, and hand jives.
And next week they'll all be different.
A few kids like Jimmy and Ann Marie
Know all the latest dances.

They look so good
The rest of us are afraid
To try to do them,
We just stand around and watch.

I'm only going to do the slow dances.
The only problem is that some of them
Start slow and then get fast.
I don't think Becky will like the "broken bobblehead."

Current Events

Mrs. McGann says to really understand events,
We should read three newspapers every day.
The New York Times, Manchester Union Leader
And *Christian Science Monitor.*

She says the *Times* and *Union Leader*
Will talk about different political views,
And the *Christian Science Monitor*
Is best for international news.

None of these papers ever seem to agree.
And they make me want to take a nap.
I can see why the country never gets anything done.
Everyone is either fighting or sleeping.

The Dance

The dance didn't turn out so good.
When I got out of the car
To pick up Becky
I stepped in dog stuff.

I had on my new white bucks.
The dog stuff was pretty noticeable
So I scraped my shoes off on the steps.
Becky stepped in it when she came out.

We tried to get it all off
But when we got in the car
We could still smell it.
Dad made us get out and try again.

It was a good thing it was a sock hop.
But Becky was still pretty mad.
She said only an idiot
Would wipe dog stuff on her steps.

Billy didn't help. He told Becky
Her perfume smelled like farm animals.
She still had some on her socks.
I called Dad to take us home.

Basketball

I tried out for the basketball team today.
I can beat almost everyone in "horse."
That's because I learned to shoot
Jump shots with either hand.

I made 20 of 25 jumpers
From outside the top of the key
But I didn't even make it
Past the first cut.

Mr. Matters said I was too short.
He said I would get trampled
And never get a shot off.
I told him I was still growing.

He only wants kids
Who are five feet six or taller.
That seems like a dumb way to pick a team.
Most of them can't shoot.

Billy said it makes sense in a way.
If none of them can shoot
Then they need tall kids to rebound,
So they can get more shots.

After Basketball

I was pretty upset
About not making the basketball team.
I asked Dad
How tall he thought I would be.

He said I was pretty much there.
That I could be a jockey
When I got older.
Mom told him to stop teasing me.

Dad isn't a lot of help
On really important stuff.
Mom said she thought
I would probably be 5′9″ or 5′10″.

Billy said being a jockey wouldn't be so bad.
He also said I could become a human cannonball.
Small guys travel farther
When they get shot out of a cannon.

I liked Mom's guess better.
At least that way
I'd be as tall as most girls
And they would dance with me.

The Dairy Queen

Sometimes we used to have ice cream
At the Dairy Queen after school got out.
All the cool kids meet there,
And they can't keep us out.

Billy and I were eating
Vanilla soft serve with sprinkles
When four of the "sculls" came in.
There weren't any seats.

So they came over and joined us.
They all had their combs out,
And Brylcreem was going everywhere.
It was pretty messy.

We started to leave
But they said if we left,
It would look like
We didn't want to sit with them.

They said we should finish our ice cream.
Billy said we would be happy
To sit with their "crew."
They didn't get it, fortunately.

Some Brylcreem got onto my ice cream
When Ducky did a massive ducktail comb.
It seemed to mix okay with the sprinkles.
We don't go to the Dairy Queen anymore.

Dress Codes

We have a pretty strict dress code at school.
Boys wear long pants and shirts with ties.
Girls wear dresses or skirts with blouses.
Last week there was a big scandal.

A ninth grader came in jeans and a T-shirt,
His girlfriend came in a short skirt and see-through blouse.
All the kids were applauding.
Miss Buxby was not pleased.

They were sent home to change.
The next day a lot of the older boys wore T-shirts and jeans
And some girls wore T-shirts.
Woodenhead called the Superintendent.

They had a meeting with some of the parents,
Who said the dress rules made clothes too expensive.
They compromised on optional slacks for the girls,
And no ties and optional jeans for the boys.

How come the cheerleaders
Can wear short skirts,
And the other girls can't?
Billy says the cheerleaders have the best legs.

Band Uniforms

They issued our band uniforms today.
Who designed these things?
Football players and cheerleaders
Get to wear great uniforms.

Boys and girls in band wear the same thing:
Hats with plume things sticking up,
Jackets with gold buttons and braids,
And pants with a stripe down the side.

We look like doormen
At a fancy hotel,
Or maybe the bad guys
At the Battle of the Alamo.

How would the cheerleaders feel
If they still had to wear uniforms
That were designed by old guys
From the dark ages?

There must be a rule written somewhere
That says that band people
Are always required
To look like dorks.

The Constitution

Gino is one of the "sculls."
He is considered the smart one.
Gino is taking history
In Miss Perkins' class.

They have been studying the Constitution.
Gino persuaded the "sculls"
To come to school today
With just their muscle shirts on.

Woodenhead was really mad.
The school and parents
Had just worked out a new agreement
On a dress code for us.

The "sculls" said it was their right.
Gino had just studied history
And the Bill of Rights clearly says
They have a right to bare arms.

Braindead Baxter

Sometimes you get a teacher
Who just doesn't have a clue.
Braindead Baxter is one of those.
She's our art teacher.

She can never remember anyone's name,
And messed up the seating chart
The first day of class.
Mom got a note from her in October.

She had me missing from class for six weeks.
Arnold's buddy, Jeremy, had been skipping class
To go out back for a smoke,
And he was listed as having 100% attendance.

Somehow, Braindead is giving me "A's"
On all my projects, but marking me absent
For all my classes.
Even Woodenhead thought this was strange.

Eventually, Braindead and Woodenhead got together
And figured it out that, on attendance,
Jeremy was me,
and I was Jeremy.

Mom says our nicknames for the teachers
Are not very respectful,
But in this case,
Her's might be justified.

Singing at Assembly

Mrs. Wildman, our music teacher,
Asked me to sing "God Bless America"
For our Columbus Day assembly.
I said I would do it.

Then she said Snobby Donna
Was going to be my accompanist.
I knew that was trouble.
The Snob smiled at me and waved.

At the assembly when my turn came,
She started playing the introduction
To "America the Beautiful,"
So that's what I sang.

Afterwards, Mrs. Wildman was pretty upset.
She asked why we changed the song.
Snobby Donna said I told her to play that.
Everybody believes Snobby Donna.

Mrs. Wildman said next time
Stick with the program,
If there is a next time.
I think she's going to give me a "C."

Relationships

It's hard to keep track
Of all the relationships in seventh grade.
Nobody can make up their mind
About who they like.

Mary Jane and her boyfriend
Have broken up and gotten back together
About six times in two months.
The bulletin board has a space for their status.

People can be "dating," or "going steady."
Becoming a "couple" is a big step up.
That involves exchanging rings
Or the girl wears his letter jacket.

"Couples" are practically married,
They only break up once or twice a year.
"Going steady" can change weekly or monthly.
"Dating" is sort of day to day.

The only way you know
Who is actually doing what,
Is to ask one of the girls.
They know everyone's status.

They have some kind of secret network
That relays news instantly.
You can always tell something has happened,
When they all start talking at once.

Kleenex and Potatoes

Billy said Irma told him
That a lot of the girls
Stuff Kleenex in their bras
To make themselves look more mature.

That didn't seem fair.
What can guys do?
We were getting way behind
In trying to look mature.

Billy's brother Dave told him
He could try stuffing a potato down there.
I tried that at home,
It doesn't work with boxer shorts.

I told Mom I needed briefs.
She got me some briefs,
But an Idaho potato looks weird.
Maine potatoes look a little better.

I tried walking to school with one,
But it kept shifting around down there,
And it's not good when it gets in back.
Maybe I should stuff Kleenex instead.

Bananas

Billy and I decided
That the potato thing wasn't going to work.
So we tried out a banana
When we were over at Billy's house.

His sister saw us walking around,
And ratted us out to her mom.
As soon as she stopped laughing,
She told us, no bananas.

It was pretty embarrassing
That she was laughing at us.
If we were sensitive kids,
We might have had emotional damage.

It's probably just as well, however.
We would have been trashed pretty bad
If the guys had seen us pulling out a banana,
When getting ready for gym.

Big Molly's Revenge

Big Molly punched out Dennis today.
Dennis has a big mouth.
He's always talking about people
When they aren't around.

He was telling fat jokes about her
In the locker room.
Billy told Irma one of the jokes.
Irma told Big Molly about Dennis.

She walked up to Dennis
In the hall before homeroom period,
And nailed him with a right cross.
She never said a word.

I think Miss Buxby saw it,
But she pretended she didn't.
Vengence is swift in seventh grade.
I'm glad I didn't box Big Molly.

High School Football

The senior high had a football game today.
They haven't won a game in two years,
And most of the team's best players
Graduated last year.

I play saxophone in the junior high band.
Senior high band is so small
They decided to let the junior high
Play in it for football games.

Without us they could only make one letter.
But when we combine
We can make SHS on the field.
That really encourages the football team.

We got beat 28–0 today,
But halftime was pretty exciting.
A majorette threw a baton way up
And it landed on Malcolm who plays the sousaphone.

He wasn't expecting it
And fell on two trumpeters
Who knocked over the bass drummer.
The crowd gave us the biggest cheer of the day.

Awards

Snobby Donna and I got awards today.
Some kind of book that dares us
To be better people.
I hope she reads it.

They took our picture
And it was pretty embarrassing.
She was holding the book
Right in front of my face.

The photographer said to do another
And look like we like each other.
She gave me a kiss on the cheek
And he used the picture.

Now Billy sings the "kissing tree" song
Whenever he sees me,
And Snobby Donna tells everyone
What a great "cheek kisser" I am.

The Kissing Fight

When Mom saw the picture in the paper
She thought it was cute.
There is nothing worse
Than being called cute by your mother.

I told her we were sworn enemies
And I needed to plot my revenge.
She said I should give her a big smooch
Right in front of the whole class.

I ran away screaming,
But then I thought about it.
I asked Billy what he thought.
He said he would kill anyone who did that.

I was pretty sure Snobby Donna wouldn't kill me.
It would look bad on her college application.
So I kissed her on the forehead
Right before math class.

She punched me in the stomach.
She's a pretty good puncher.
I couldn't breathe for about five minutes.
We both got detention.

It was her first detention ever.
I told all the kids
That she was a great forehead kisser.
Maybe she will kill me.

Butchy Talks with Arnold

Arnold has been even meaner lately.
Last week he took my whole lunch
And then gave me a noogie anyway.
He did the same thing to Marvin.

Butchy dropped out of school over the summer.
He works in the lumberyard now.
Butchy and I were friends from elementary school.
I dropped by and told him about Arnold.

He said he would come by after school
And have a little talk with Arnold.
He must have had a good talk.
Arnold had a big black eye yesterday.

But he didn't take any lunches or give anyone noogies.
I asked Mom to make oatmeal cookies,
And brought them to Butchy.
Butchy said he just talked to him.

When I told Mom
That Butchy and I had solved the Arnold problem,
She wondered how Arnold got the black eye,
If Butchy just talked to him.

The Becky Fight

I don't think Becky and I
Are dating any more.
She was still upset about the dog stuff
And the kissing fight with Snobby Donna.

I'm starting to think Dad was right.
It might be a good idea
To stay away from girls
Until I'm twenty-one.

They basically drive me crazy.
They don't think in a normal way,
Talk about stupid stuff like feelings,
And get upset over almost anything.

I tried to make up with Becky
By telling her that Arnold said
She looked really good in the locker room.
I'm getting punched a lot lately.

Report Cards

We got our report cards yesterday.
I got "A's" in everything
Except "C's" in French, music and gym.
Snobby Donna got all "A's."

Mom asked me how
I could get a "C" in music.
I said it was Snobby Donna's fault.
Mom said I blame her for everything.

I suddenly knew what to do
With my Junior Mints box.
I wrapped it with a pretty ribbon
And wrote "congratulations" on the card.

I put it on her desk
Before she got to homeroom.
The leeches had thawed out pretty good
Before she opened it.

She screamed and threw the box.
It landed on Big Molly.
Molly tried to run but slipped on a leech
And knocked over Alice's science project.

Alice's ants were everywhere.
Somebody ratted me out
So I got more detention,
But it was worth it.

Making up with Becky

I tried to make up with Becky again.
I brought her an apple
From my lunch,
And asked if we could talk.

I said I was very sorry
About all the stuff I'd done wrong lately.
She asked about Snobby Donna
And I told her we were sworn enemies.

Things were going pretty well,
And then I got carried away.
I said I made it up that Arnold said
She looked good in the locker room.

She threw the apple at me
And walked away.
It's hard to understand what girls want.
I don't think we're getting back together.

The Debate

We had a debate in speech class today.
Mrs. Pickerel picked me to debate Snobby Donna.
The class got to pick the topic, and they chose
"Are girls smarter then boys?"

Snobby Donna argued the pros.
She said girls were smarter in a crisis,
They don't try to solve everything by violence,
And they get better grades than boys.

I responded point by point.
I said if that were true,
How come she totally panicked
At the sight of a few dead leeches.

And why did she resolve our kissing fight
By punching me in the stomach.
I also took exception to the grade thing.
There were extenuating circumstances.

I was unduly distracted in French class.
She sabotaged me in music,
And I said she would have got a "C" in gym too
If she had to do the rope climb.

The kids voted that I lost the debate.
(There are more girls in the class.)
Even worse, Snobby Donna said
She could do the rope climb easy.

The Rope Climb

Billy said I was in big trouble.
Irma told him that Snobby Donna
Was one of the best athletes in gym.
She can even do a pull-up.

Mr. Foster said he would give her a chance
To do the rope climb.
Then he looked over and smiled at me.
I always knew he hated me.

A bunch of the kids came after school to watch.
The Pep Squad came out to cheer for her.
Becky was even there.
She's dating Wally now.

Snobby Donna climbed the rope
In twenty-two seconds.
Her time was faster than Arnold's.
I need to move to South America.

Rope Climb—The Day After

There was a message on the school bulletin board.
It said "Rope Climb Results"
Donna—22 seconds
Glenn—Forever

Then it listed all the other boys she beat.
I am total toast at school.
The boys hate me for embarrassing them
And the girls think I'm a nerd.

They stopped calling me "cheesehead."
Now I'm the "rope-a-dope."
I never thought "cheesehead" would be the good name.
I hate seventh grade.

I figured things couldn't get much worse.
Then this afternoon, Big Molly
Put up a blow-up of the gym picture
With a red arrow pointing to "rope-a-dope's butt."

What Girls Want

I asked Billy what he thought girls wanted.
He said they like lots of ice cream.
If you don't get them ice cream
They get very cranky.

I think Irma likes ice cream.
I wasn't sure if that was universal, however.
Billy sometimes lacks subtlety
In his approach to things.

So I asked Mom.
She said girls like boys who are
Smart, kind and have a sense of humor.
Mom hasn't been to school in a while.

The popular boys in school
Seem to be dumb, mean and tall.
I guess Mom meant girls in the olden days,
Before they became crazy.

Second Base

Billy said he almost got to second base.
He took Irma to the movies.
They snuck up to the balcony
And started kissing and fooling around.

Then the problem developed.
He couldn't figure out
How to unhook her bra
With only one hand.

Those things are pretty complicated
And they always put the hooks in the back.
Why don't they put them in front
Where you can get at them?

Billy has an older sister.
He's going to "borrow" one of her bras
So we can practice unhooking it
With just one hand.

Bras

Billy's sister is seventeen
So he was able to get a good bra
That we could practice on.
We put it around the back of a chair.

We put another chair next to it.
It was pretty tricky.
Maybe the chair was too big,
It made a tight fit.

When Billy finally got it undone
It almost put his eye out.
He was leaning in
And it came off fast.

We finally got the hang of it,
But it took a lot of practice.
I hope they don't make them
With more than two hooks.

Other Thoughts on Girl Stuff

When Billy was "borrowing" his sister's bra
He said he found something else in there.
He said his sister has
Some really weird stuff.

One thing had hooks in back like a bra,
But then the front part
Hung down with two long straps
Attached to it.

We were thinking maybe
They were like suspenders for girls,
To help them keep their pants up
When they didn't wear a belt.

Then we looked it up in the Sears catalog.
They actually use it to keep their stockings up.
Girls have some pretty strange things,
And they all hook in the back.

The Sex Lecture

We had a sex lecture in school today.
Miss Buxby and Lead Belly did it.
I guess they picked them
Because they were the oldest.

They said we were too young for sex,
And should save ourselves for marriage.
They also said we should only have sex
If we want to have babies.

Then they told us about the risks
Of all the diseases from sex.
They tried to scare us
But I don't think it did much good.

None of the kids could imagine
Anyone having sex with either one of them,
So we decided they were probably
Making it all up.

They had a question and answer session afterwards.
I asked them what "mens truation" was.
A lot of the kids laughed.
Miss Buxby said that was enough questions.

I don't think she knows either.

French Kissing

Some of the kids at school
Were talking about French kissing.
I asked Billy if he knew
What that was.

He said it was kissing in French class.
But we decided to ask his big brother.
Dave is sixteen and knows
All about that stuff.

Dave said it's when you kiss
And stick your tongue
Down the girl's throat,
To show how sophisticated you are.

He gave us some advice.
Never eat a tuna fish sandwich
Before you French kiss.
Some things are best not shared.

The whole thing seems pretty gross.
Why would you want to do that?
Two tongues in one mouth
Sounds pretty crowded.

The Real Sex Lecture

After the school sex lecture
I started worrying about disease.
Someone said you could get it
Just sitting on the toilet seat.

Now I always put paper on the toilet seat.
We decided to ask Dave
About all the sex disease stuff.
He said you can only get "mono" from kissing.

He also told us about condoms.
They help protect against disease.
I asked if you needed to use them
To get to second base.

He gave me a look like I was an idiot.
Then he showed us
How to put one on a banana.
It looked pretty complicated just getting it opened.

I'm a little bit disillusioned.
I said I found one on my Dad's bedside table
And he said it was for his big toe.
Now I find out they're for this banana stuff.

Dunking Mr. Foster

We had a fundraiser near Halloween.
It was to raise money
For the sports teams
And uniforms for the band.

Mr. Foster volunteered for the dunking chair.
He has to sit in a chair above a pool of water,
And if we hit the target with a baseball,
He gets dunked.

I have a really good throwing arm.
I pitched a no-hitter in Little League.
I have almost perfect control,
And throw pretty hard.

I really wanted to get even with him
For putting me in the ring with Henry,
And letting Snobby Donna do the rope climb.
I had some money saved from my candy route.

I gave Billy 10 cents to buy
Two big bags of ice cubes.
He snuck around behind the pool,
And poured them in.

I waited about ten minutes
And then paid 25 cents for three baseballs.
I hit the target all three times.
I could tell he was tired of hitting the water.

Then Marvin bought me three more balls.
I dunked him twice more.
Mr. Foster looked cold and wet.
Revenge is sweet.

Charles Atlas

I was tired of being a rope-a-dope,
And I saw an ad
On the back of one of my
Superman comic books.

Charles Atlas said I could become
A big muscle guy,
If I just took his course.
I sent in for a free booklet.

I didn't want to be the 97 pound weakling.
I was fed up with being too short
And not being able to climb
The stupid rope.

Billy said it wouldn't work.
There would always be big guys
Who also took the course,
To kick sand in my face.

He said an easier way
Is to stop exercising,
And eat a lot of jelly donuts, fried chicken
And Baby Ruth candy bars.

Then I could become the anchor man,
In the tug-of-war. I would be a hero,
And all I would have to do
Is sit on the stupid rope.

68

The Halloween Dance

Billy and I didn't have dates
For the Halloween dance,
So we decided to go stag
And see who was dating who.

Snobby Donna was there with Richie.
That was a big surprise.
Richie looks like a movie star
But is dumber than a fence post.

In history class, Mr. Benson
Asked him who was Abraham Lincoln.
He said that he invented
The Lincoln automobile.

In Boy Scouts, we convinced him
To go on a snipe hunt.
He came back with Mrs. Emerson's
Little Shar-Pei , Alexander, in a bag.

The dog was traumatized
And started urinating in her house.
Mrs. Emerson wouldn't let us play
Capture the flag in her woods anymore.

I figured Snobby Donna and Richie deserved each other.
I wished them a nice broom ride.
The Snob complimented me on my scary costume.
I wasn't wearing one.

Locker Inspection

We had a surprise locker inspection today.
All the homeroom teachers
Had each of us open our lockers
To make sure we only had authorized stuff.

Miss Buxby found a *Playboy*
In Arnold's locker. It was his father's.
She confiscated it, and sent a note to his mother.
His father hadn't seen it yet.

They found a pair of girl's panties
In Daniel's locker.
He says they were a souvenir.
No one believes him.

Lead Belly opened Billy's locker.
That was a big mistake. He almost barfed.
Wrapped in some really ripe gym clothes,
They found a three-week-old fishstick.

I asked Billy why he was saving
A three-week-old fish stick.
He said Irma gave it to him for Tipper,
But then he forgot about it.

They only found a dead cockroach in mine.
He must have gotten out of the matchbox
We brought to the cafeteria
For Big Molly.

B-Flat

Well Snobby Donna has done it again.
Miss Perfect is perfect in something else.
Mrs. Wildman was very impressed
When she did a test with the class.

She began to play notes on the piano,
And asked if anyone could identify them.
Snobby Donna knew them all.
And she knew all the chords too.

Mrs. Wildman said that was amazing.
Apparently Miss Perfect has perfect pitch.
I think I am going to do
A perfect puke.

Even the other kids in class
Were rolling their eyes.
Then Henry let out a huge belch.
Snobby Donna said "B-Flat."

Even I started laughing
At that one.
That's the first time she's ever showed
She has a sense of humor.

Washed Up

My career as a singer is over.
Mrs. Wildman had me scheduled to sing
White Christmas for the Christmas program.
But in rehearsals, my voice started cracking.

It cracks at weird times,
And I don't know when it will happen.
I used to sing on the Newsboys Show in Boston
And at a lot of different events.

Now, I'm all washed up.
Mrs. Wildman said my voice might be okay,
When it gets finished changing,
But I'm done as a soloist.

I thought turning thirteen would be great,
But now my only claim to fame, all my dreams,
Have been shattered.
I'm just a rope-a-dope.

I heard that child stars
Fall apart when they're no longer famous.
Billy said I'd be okay
Because I was never that famous or a star.

He said I should be grateful.
Girls don't like it
When your voice
Is higher than theirs.

Bad Breath

Mr. Stuben is one of the eighth grade science teachers.
His nickname is "the Squirrel Killer."
The kids call him "Squeakey" for short.
We asked Billy's older brother how he got the name.

Dave said it's because he has really bad breath.
I can verify that's true.
He stopped me in the hall once.
It's worse than Henry's farts.

Apparently he opened a window in class one day
And a squirrel in a nearby tree
Keeled over dead.
They found its body in the grass.

Mom said it was probably some gas
From an experiment that killed the squirrel.
But after meeting him in the hall,
I believe it was his breath.

The rumor is that
When he needs animals for dissection,
He just goes out in the woods
And coughs a lot.

The Orchestra

Because our high school is small,
They let the junior high kids
Also play in the orchestra.
We have a famous conductor.

Mr. Tarley plays first violin
In the Boston Symphony.
We aren't quite up to that level,
But sometimes we sound pretty good.

They already have a better piano player
And better saxophone players,
So he uses me in the percussion section.
I play anything no one else plays.

I have a lot of fun with it.
I play xylophone, glockenspiel, bells,
Chimes, bass drum and cymbals.
I don't have to carry anything home.

I was a soloist last night at the concert.
I played chimes in the "Bells of St. Mary."
I thought this might make the girls forget
That I was a rope-a dope.

Billy said it really didn't help.
A music nerd is about as bad.
He said girls don't dig music nerds
Until they become rock stars.

Puppies and People

Billy said it was too hard dating girls.
Irma broke up with him.
She said he needed better smelling sneakers.
She also didn't like his French kiss.

He said puppies had it
A lot easier than people.
I thought about that for a while
And then mentioned some problems.

I said puppies have to meet each other
By rubbing noses and smelling rear ends.
Then they still have to find a human
To clean up their poop and feed them.

On the other hand, Billy pointed out,
They don't have to do rope climbs,
Speak French or have homework.
I may be losing this debate.

I still don't like the idea
Of having to smell the rear ends
Of everyone I meet.
Especially the "Mad Farter."

The Old Guy

Billy and I were coming home from school today.
We were down by the E. L. Patch buildings when
We found an old guy
Wandering around in his underpants.

He said he needed to get to Chicago.
He wanted to catch the next train.
There was a closed boxcar on the siding
And he was trying to get into it.

He said he would have driven,
But he forgot his license,
And couldn't find his car.
He thinks someone stole it.

We figured he would have a hard time making it
To Chicago in an old boxcar.
We also wondered if it was unusual
For old guys to be outside in their underpants.

My Grandpa didn't usually do that,
Except the time he was getting the paper
And accidentally locked himself out.
Billy said old guys do lots of weird stuff.

We went up to the Patch's office
And they called the police.
It turned out the old guy
Was an escapee from the old people's home.

I guess we're heroes
For helping capture the old guy.
He didn't seem to mind,
They told him tonight was Bingo night.

Batman vs Superman

Billy and I had a major argument yesterday.
We were coming home from school.
I told him I thought it would be neat
To be Superman.

I said I loved all his super powers.
He could climb ropes and fly
And was stronger than anyone.
I especially liked the x-ray vision thing.

He said that was okay
But Batman was better.
Batman had lots of money,
A great car and a fancy mansion.

He said Batman could get all the girls,
Because he was rich and handsome,
And he didn't have to live alone
In an ice house in the Arctic.

I said Superman would beat Batman easy.
He said Batman would buy some Kryptonite.
Finally we decided Batman should dump Robin
And form a partnership with Superman.

They would be great crimefighters
And Batman could get Superman dates.
Then they could fly off to Monte Carlo or Tahiti
And have super parties.

Where the Girls Are

Billy joined the Future Teachers of America.
I told him I couldn't imagine
Him becoming a teacher.
Billy looked at me like I was a dummy.

He said he wasn't
Going to be a teacher.
He was joining it because
Almost all girls were in it.

After breaking up with Irma,
He said he needed new horizons.
And there were lots
Of new horizons in the club.

I said, based on that stupid logic,
I should sign up for ballet lessons.
He said that was a good idea,
I'd look cute in a tutu.

I still haven't figured out seventh grade.
Boy-girl stuff is a lot trickier.
Before, we mostly just ignored
Or tormented each other.

Now, the only thing I know for sure,
Is I hope I start shaving soon.
That seems to answer
A lot of the questions.

The Snowball Fight

When it started to snow
During fifth period, I smiled.
It was a pretty wet snow
And was accumulating fast.

Unless you live more than two miles away
You have to walk to school.
I figured I had a great chance
For revenge on Snobby Donna.

I skipped last period
And made a good supply of snowballs.
I was ready when she came out
But, unfortunately, her father picked her up.

I had to use up the snowballs,
So I started a fight with Arnold.
We had a pretty good battle going.
Arnold and three friends against Billy, Wally and me.

I nailed Arnold four times
Before Lead Belly broke it up.
Something seemed to change after the fight.
Arnold smiled and waved at the end.

Arnold

I think my problems with Arnold
May be over.
He said he wants me on his side
In the next snowball fight.

Arnold doesn't seem as angry anymore.
Billy said he heard in accounting class
That his father used to smack him around,
But that now his father is in jail.

It seems strange that someone
Would feel better when his father
Gets sent to jail.
I'm glad my dad isn't in jail.

Braces

Billy got braces last week.
His dentist said he has an overbite.
He may need to wear them
For a year or two, maybe longer.

His dentist is the Snob's father, Dr. Dynan.
He told Billy he knew
That he was the other "chipmunk boy."
Then he gave him the gas.

When Billy woke up,
His mouth looked like the grill
On the new Chryslers.
He said he was wired up tight.

He told me he was worried
That none of the girls
Would want to kiss him,
Because they might get injured.

I told him maybe
The French kissing was out.
But that hadn't worked too well anyway.
Irma thought he was trying to kill her.

I think it could be a problem.
He's pretty disgusting after he eats.
Sometimes half his meal is hanging off his braces.
The girl would have to be awfully hungry.

Billy's Accident

Billy was in hall traffic yesterday.
Everybody was rushing and it was crowded.
He got tripped from behind
And stumbled into Paulina.

He didn't fall down completely.
He sort of caught himself on Paulina.
His braces got stuck
On the back of her skirt.

Paulina is the head cheerleader.
She's a ninth grader.
She's a "couple" with Bubba Bailey,
The captain of the football team.

Billy was stuck to her behind.
It took them a long time
To get his braces freed up.
Bubba and Pauline were not happy.

When they finally got loose,
Billy still had some wool
Sticking out of his braces.
Billy's lucky to be alive.

Drugs

Two weeks ago, there was a guy
In the woods behind the school.
He was selling stuff
To some ninth graders.

The police had talked to us
At assembly a while ago,
About the danger of drugs,
And to stay away from those guys.

Denard was one of the ninth graders.
He called us over and warned us,
That if we told anyone,
He would kill us.

We said we were taking
A shortcut to the ballfield,
And hadn't seen anything.
We didn't tell anyone.

Thursday, the police arrested the guy,
And Denard got kicked off
The school football team.
Denard thinks we ratted him out.

Nobody wants to sit near us.
They are worried they might be killed too.
The police were right
About the dangers of drugs.

Saved by the Paper

Our lives were saved when the local paper
Wrote a story about the arrest.
One of the ninth graders who took the drugs,
Wound up in the hospital.

His parents made him tell
Where he got the drugs.
The kid is okay
But he's being sent to private school.

Denard is still not a happy person.
I think he would like to kill someone.
We're being very careful
To stay out of his way.

The Truce

Mr. Meekers assigned us a major science project
That was due in a month.
We had to work together
With our lab partners.

Snobby Donna and I don't talk much in lab.
I just let her do whatever she wants
In our lab experiments
While I stand back and watch.

I can't believe we're stuck
Having to work together.
The project is half our grade
So we'll have to call a truce.

She said I would have to help on this.
I couldn't just sit back
And check her out.
That started another fight, although it was true.

We finally agreed to actually work together
For the sake of the grade.
But we reaffirmed that afterwards,
We would be sworn enemies.

The Project

Even though I didn't help in lab,
I am really smart in science.
Snobby Donna is pretty good too.
I figured we had a chance to get a good grade.

I decided to refer to her just as "Donna"
Until the end of our project.
She is really good at drawing and art
And I'm pretty good at shop.

We decided to get together after school
and went to her house.
She gave me some lemonade,
And her mom called me "chipmunk boy."

I guess they're not over that yet.
We finally decided to do a project
Where we drilled a hole through the earth,
And dropped a ball in to see where it would go.

That was my idea.
One of the things I always wondered about.
Donna thought it was pretty weird,
But that it would be really different.

Meeting at My House

The next time we met,
We went to my house.
My mom said, "Oh, you're the girl
Who's so good at the rope climb."

My mom is really mean sometimes.
She thought it was pretty funny.
Donna didn't say anything,
A wise move considering the look I gave Mom.

We went to Dad's study
And decided I would make the globe
And get the magnets, rails and stuff.
She would do the charts, drawings and writing.

It actually turned into a fun project.
I'm having trouble
Continuing to hate her.
I'll have to talk to Billy.

We Discuss Snobby Donna

Billy said I needed to pull it together.
We've been hating Snobby Donna
Since 4th grade.
We even swore vows.

I said that's a long time
To hate someone.
Maybe we should give her
Another chance.

Billy reminded me
That I was a "rope-a-dope,
And that I got a "C" in music.
I said she was pretty cute.

We decided to think about it.
Does cuteness offset
Someone being Miss Perfect,
And making me a "rope-a-dope"?

It's a tough decision.

Menstruation

Yikes! I finally found out
What menstruation is.
No wonder girls
Are always cranky.

Nobody would tell me
So I asked Mom.
She's the only one around here
Who knows anything.

She also said there's something
Called menopause.
I don't understand what "men"
Have to do with any of this stuff.

Men get blamed for everything.

The Project Grade

We got an "A+" on our science project.
Mr. Meeker said it was one of the most
Interesting and unusual ones
He had ever seen.

We were both pretty happy.
Donna even gave me a hug.
I said, maybe we shouldn't be enemies anymore.
She said that would be okay.

Things are actually improving for me.
I'm now known as a nerdy science guy,
Instead of just a nerd.
I still can't do the rope climb.

Billy said it was alright
To make up with Snobby Donna.
He said we'd find more people to hate
When we got to eighth grade.

Donna's Recital

I went to Donna's Christmas recital yesterday.
Almost all the people there were parents
Of the kids performing.
Donna saw me and came over afterwards.

We went downstairs
And had some punch and cookies.
I told her
That she played the piano really well.

Her father came over and said,
"So you're the `chipmunk boy.'
Come and see me sometime at the office,
I'd really like to work on your teeth."

That didn't seem like a good idea.
He had a strange look in his eye.
I guess it took them a long time
To catch the chipmunk.

I hope Donna didn't tell them about the leeches.
They already seem a little peeved.
They might not be my biggest supporters,
If I invite Donna to the Valentine's Day dance.

Conclusion

After four months, I think I am finally
Getting so I understand seventh grade.
You go from the top of the heap in grade school
To the bottom side of a meadow muffin.

There are three basic rules:
Don't get Miss Buxby mad,
Stay out of Denard's way,
And don't try to understand girls.

You also need to understand,
That homework is there to make you miserable,
Gym is there to make sure you stay miserable,
And French teaches you miserable in another language.

It's also a time
When your body does weird stuff,
To insure that you remain confused
And embarrassed throughout the year.

The real key to survival
Is to remember that you are now a teenager.
You will soon rule the world.
Suffering prepares you for greater things.

Next year, you will be in eighth grade,
And you can look forward
To making those worthless seventh graders
Even more miserable.

About the Author

GLENN K. CURRIE is a humorist, essayist and poet. He graduated from Dartmouth College in 1965 and served in the U.S. Navy from 1965 to 1969. He worked in corporate America from 1970 to 1986, during which time he traveled extensively, primarily in the Middle East. He and his family returned to New Hampshire and settled in Concord in 1986, where he maintained a private consulting business and became a freelance writer.

He was a regular contributor to the *Concord Monitor* for two decades and has also been an occasional contributor to *New Hampshire Magazine*, and has written for other magazines and newspapers over the last thirty years.

Currie has previously published three collections of poetry, *Daydreams* (2004), *Riding in Boxcars* (2006), and *In the Cat's Eye* (2009). In 2011 he published his first collection of essays, *Granite Grumblings: Life in the "Live Free or Die" State*, a humorous look at life in New Hampshire. *Surviving Seventh Grade* is his second young adult book, and includes many of the characters in *A Boy's First Diary*. Further information is available on his website: www.snapscreenpress.com.

Heights